WAIT UNTIL DARK

W9-CKP-815

TALES OF SUSPENSE BY
J.B. STAMPER

SCHOLASTIC INC.
New York   Toronto   London   Auckland   Sydney
Mexico City   New Delhi   Hong Kong

COVER ILLUSTRATION BY
TIM JESSELL

"The Corpse's Revenge," "Mummies," and "Graveyard Dare" © 1993 by J.B. Stamper
were first published in NIGHT FRIGHTS by Scholastic Inc.
"The Jigsaw Puzzle" and "Phobia" © 1977 by J.B. Stamper
were first published in TALES FOR THE MIDNIGHT HOUR by Scholastic Inc.
"Better Late Than Never" and "The Gecko" © 1991 by J.B. Stamper
were first published in EVEN MORE TALES FOR THE MIDNIGHT HOUR
by Scholastic Inc.

Compilation copyright © 1999 by Scholastic Inc.
Cover illustration copyright © 1999 by Scholastic Inc.
All rights reserved. Published by Scholastic Inc.
Printed in the U.S.A.

ISBN 0-439-05689-6

SCHOLASTIC, READ 180, and associated logos and designs are
trademarks and/or registered trademarks of Scholastic Inc.
LEXILE is a trademark of MetaMetrics, Inc.

15   14   13   23   07   08   09

TABLE OF CONTENTS

THE JIGSAW PUZZLE

It was on the top shelf of an old bookcase, covered with dust and barely visible. Lisa decided she had to find out what it was. Of all the things in the old junk shop, it aroused her curiosity most. She had looked through old books, prints, and postcards for hours. Nothing had caught her interest. Now the old box, high and out of reach, intrigued her.

She looked around for the old man who ran the store. But he had gone into the back room. She saw a stepladder across the room and brought it over to the bookcase. It shook on the uneven floorboards as she climbed to the top step.

Lisa patted her hand along the surface of the top shelf, trying to find the box. The dirt was thick and gritty on the board. Then she touched the box. It was made of cardboard. The cardboard was cold and soft from being in the damp room for such a long time. She lifted the box down slowly, trying to steady her balance on the stepladder.

As the side of the box reached her eye level, she could read the words: 500 PIECES.

She sat the box down on top of the stepladder and climbed down a few steps. Then she blew away some of the dust that had accumulated on the lid. It billowed up around her with a musty, dead odor. But now she could make out a few more words on top of the box:

THE STRANGEST
JIGSAW PUZZLE
IN THE WORLD

There were other words underneath that, but they had been rubbed off the cardboard lid. The big picture on the cover had been curiously damaged. Lisa could make out areas of light and dark. It looked as though the scene might be in a room. But most of the picture had been scratched off the cardboard box, probably by a sharp instrument.

The mysterious nature of the jigsaw puzzle made it even more appealing to Lisa. She decided she would buy it. The lid was taped down securely; that probably meant that all the pieces would be there. As she carefully climbed down the stepladder, holding the box in both hands, Lisa smiled to herself. It was quite a find, just the sort of thing she had always hoped to discover while rummaging through secondhand stores.

Mr. Tuborg, the owner of the store, came out of the back room as she was walking up to his sales desk. He looked curiously at the box when Lisa set it down.

"And where did you find that?" he asked her.

Lisa pointed to where she had set up the stepladder. "It was on top of that bookcase. You could barely see it from the floor."

"Well, I've never seen it before, that's for sure," Mr. Tuborg said. "I can't imagine how you found it."

Lisa was more pleased than ever about her find. She felt as though the puzzle had been hiding up there, waiting for her to discover it. She paid Mr. Tuborg the 25 cents he asked for the puzzle and then wrapped it carefully in the newspapers he gave her to take it home in.

It was late on a Saturday afternoon. Lisa lived alone in a small room in an old apartment house. She had no plans for Saturday night. Now she decided to spend the whole evening working on the puzzle. She stopped at a delicatessen and bought some meat, bread, and cheese for sandwiches. She would eat while she put the puzzle together.

As soon as she had climbed the flight of stairs to her room and put away the groceries, Lisa cleaned off the big table in the center of the room. She set the box down on it.

THE STRANGEST
JIGSAW PUZZLE
IN THE WORLD

Lisa read the words again. She wondered what they could mean. How strange could a jigsaw puzzle be?

The tape that held the lid down was still strong. Lisa got out a kitchen knife to slice through it. When she lifted the cover off the box, a musty smell came from inside. But the jigsaw pieces all looked in good condition. Lisa picked one up. The color was faded, but the picture was clear. She could see the shape of a finger in the piece. It looked like a woman's finger.

Lisa sat down and started to lay out the pieces, top side up, on the large table. As she took them from the box, she sorted out the flat-edged pieces from the inside pieces. Every so often, she would recognize something in one of the pieces. She saw some blonde hair, a window pane, and a small vase. There was a lot of wood texture in the pieces, plus what looked like wallpaper. Lisa noticed that the wallpaper in the puzzle looked a lot like the wallpaper in her own room. She wondered if her wallpaper was as old as the jigsaw puzzle. It would be an incredible coincidence, but it could be the same.

By the time Lisa had all of the pieces laid out on the table, it was 6:30. She got up and made herself a sandwich. Already, her back was beginning to hurt a little from leaning over the table. But she couldn't stay away from the puzzle. She went back to the table and set her sandwich down beside her. It was always like that when she did jigsaws. Once she started, she couldn't stop until the puzzle was all put together.

She began to sort out the edge pieces according to

their coloring. There were dark brown pieces, whitish pieces, the wallpaper pieces, and some pieces that seemed to be like glass—perhaps a window. As she slowly ate her sandwich, Lisa pieced together the border. When she was finished, she knew she had been right about the setting of the picture when she had first seen the puzzle. It was a room. One side of the border was wallpaper. Lisa decided to fill that in first. She was curious about its resemblance to her own wallpaper.

She gathered all the pieces together that had the blue and lilac flowered design. As she fit the pieces together, it became clear that the wallpaper in the puzzle was identical to the wallpaper in her room. Lisa glanced back and forth between the puzzle and her wall. It was an exact match.

By now it was 8:30. Lisa leaned back in her chair. Her back was stiff. She looked over at her window. The night was black outside. Lisa got up and walked over to the window. Suddenly, she felt uneasy, alone in the apartment. She pulled the white shade over the window.

She paced around the room once, trying to think of something else she might do instead of finishing the puzzle. But nothing else interested her. She went back and sat down at the table.

Next she started to fill in the lower right-hand corner. There was a rug and then a chair. This part of the puzzle was very dark. Lisa noticed uneasily that the chair was the same shape as one sitting in the corner of her room. But the colors didn't seem exactly the same. Her chair was maroon. The one in the puzzle was in the shadows and seemed almost black.

Lisa continued to fill in the border toward the middle. There was more wallpaper to finish on top. The left-hand side did turn out to be a window. Through it, a half moon hung in a dark sky. But it was the bottom of the puzzle that began to bother Lisa. As the pieces fell into place, she saw a picture of a pair of legs, crossed underneath a table. They were the legs of a young woman. Lisa reached down and ran her hand along one of her legs. Suddenly, she had felt as though something was crawling up it, but it must have been her imagination.

She stared down at the puzzle. It was almost three-quarters done. Only the middle remained. Lisa glanced at the lid of the puzzle box:

THE STRANGEST
JIGSAW . . .

She shuddered.

Lisa leaned back in her chair again. Her back ached. Her neck muscles were tense and strained. She thought about quitting the puzzle. It scared her now.

She stood up and stretched. Then she looked down at the puzzle on the table. It looked different from the higher angle. Lisa was shocked by what she saw. Her body began to tremble all over.

It was unmistakable—the picture in the puzzle was of her own room. The window was placed correctly in relation to the table. The bookcase stood in its exact spot against the wall. Even the carved table legs were the same. . . .

Lisa raised her hand to knock the pieces of the puzzle apart. She didn't want to finish the strangest jigsaw puzzle in the world; she didn't want to find out what the hole in the middle of the puzzle might turn out to be.

But then she lowered her hand. Perhaps it was worse not to know. Perhaps it was worse to wait and wonder.

Lisa sank back down into the chair at the table. She fought off the fear that crept into the sore muscles of her back. Deliberately, piece by piece, she began to fill in the hole in the puzzle. She put together a picture of a table, on which lay a jigsaw puzzle. This puzzle inside the puzzle was finished. But Lisa couldn't make out what it showed. She pieced together the young woman who was sitting at the table—the young woman who was herself. As she filled in the picture, her own body slowly filled with horror and dread. It was all there in the picture . . . the vase filled with blue cornflowers, her red cardigan sweater, the wild look of fear on her own face.

The jigsaw puzzle lay before her—finished except for two adjoining pieces. They were dark pieces, ones she hadn't been able to fit into the area of the window. Lisa looked behind her. The white blind was drawn over her window. With relief, she realized that the puzzle picture was not exactly like her room. It showed the black night behind the window and a moon shining in the sky.

With trembling hands, Lisa reached for the second to last piece. She dropped it into one of the empty spaces. It seemed to be half a face, but not a human face. She reached for the last piece. She pressed it into the small hole left in the picture.

The face was complete—the face in the window. It was more horrible than anything she had ever seen, or dreamed. Lisa looked at the picture of herself in the puzzle and then back to that face.

Then she whirled around. The blind was no longer over her window. The night showed black through the window pane. A half moon hung low in the sky.

Lisa screamed . . . the face . . . it was there, too.

MUMMIES

It had sounded like such a good idea—staying overnight in the museum. But now Robbie wasn't sure. He was curled up inside his sleeping bag, right beside a cold, hard column that held up a big stone lion. Luke and Michael were right beside him. Mr. Arnold and the rest of the class were scattered around the big room where they were spending the night.

Mr. Arnold had been teaching them Egyptian history for four weeks, and they had all learned how to write hieroglyphics and how to make model pyramids. Mr. Arnold's old friend from college, Mr. Ellerby, was curator of the museum and had invited the class to spend the night there. For "atmosphere," he had said.

"Be quiet now, boys and girls," Mr. Arnold announced. "It's a great favor that Mr. Ellerby is doing for us, letting you spend the night here. I don't want any of you to leave the room, except, of course, to visit the rest room. And now, Mr. Ellerby would like to say a few words."

Michael poked Robbie in the ribs and snickered.

He'd been making fun of Mr. Ellerby all day.

Mr. Ellerby cleared his throat and looked around at all the children huddled in their sleeping bags. His voice, as Robbie remembered from earlier in the day, sounded dry and cracked—like the old mummies they'd seen in the Egyptian rooms.

"I invited you boys and girls here," he began, "so that you could imagine what it was like to live centuries ago, like the ancient Egyptians. But I want to warn you. The museum is a different place at night. I often wonder what happens in those rooms at night where the remains of the past lie so quietly during the day. I wonder if the mummies move under their centuries-old wrappings . . . and rise out of their cases. I never go into the mummy rooms of the museum at night. And I don't want you to, either."

Just then, one of the youngest girls in the class let out a frightened scream and began to cry. Robbie felt a lump rise in his own throat. Suddenly, he wanted to be home sleeping in his bed—not here in this drafty old museum with its weird statues and mummies.

Mr. Arnold rushed up to Mr. Ellerby and whispered something in his ear. Mr. Ellerby smiled nervously and then apologized to the class if he had scared them.

"I know all of you will stay out of the mummy rooms," he said. "I just wanted to make sure."

Then Mr. Arnold told everyone to go to sleep. He turned down the main lights, but left a few small lights glowing.

Robbie huddled deeper into his sleeping bag as the lights were switched off. It was almost pitch-dark in the corner where he and his friends lay. But Robbie could see the lumpy shadows of the other children sleeping on the floor of the hall. It was strange, but in the dim light, they almost looked like mummies.

Robbie woke with a start, bumping his head against the stone column he was sleeping beside. In a panic, he looked around him and saw the dim lights and huddled bodies on the floor of the museum. He'd been having a dream, a horrible dream about Mr. Ellerby taking him into the Egyptian Land of the Dead.

For long seconds, the spookily lit hall seemed no more real to Robbie than his dream had been. He couldn't understand where he was. Then, as the sleep cleared from his brain, he realized that he was in the museum. And he had a problem. He had to find a rest room.

Robbie squirmed out of his sleeping bag and crept across the cold marble floor, searching for Mr. Arnold. Mr. Arnold had said that anyone should wake him during the night if they had to go to the rest room. Robbie peered at one sleeping body after another, but none of them was Mr. Arnold. Maybe, Robbie thought, Mr. Arnold had taken someone else to the rest room. He'd probably meet them on the way.

Robbie started down the long corridor toward the rest room. It was lined with the heads of Egyptian kings, their marble eyes peering at him in the dim light. Robbie shivered. It had become colder during the night, and the cold floor beneath his stocking feet seemed to draw all the warmth out of his body.

Robbie came to a fork in the corridor that he hadn't remembered. He peered down the narrow hallway to the left and thought he saw a red EXIT sign. He turned down the hallway, even though the lighting was dimmer. He reached out his hands and felt the smooth, cold glass of a display case. There had been cases just like this in the hallway near the mummy room.

Robbie suddenly turned around and started to run. He didn't care about the rest room anymore; he just wanted to get back to the main hall where everyone else was. But as he started back down the dim hall, he suddenly walked right into a stone wall. In a panic, he felt the wall from one side of the corridor to the other. It was a dead end. Somehow, he'd gotten mixed up in the dark.

Then he saw the red glow again, the same red glow he'd thought was an EXIT sign. Robbie ran toward it until he came to a narrow door. He walked inside a room where an ancient Egyptian lamp glowed with a flickering, red flame.

The mummy room. Robbie whirled around to run. But just then, a stone slab rolled over the narrow doorway he had come through. And standing perfectly still beside the door was a mummy out of its case.

Robbie felt fear creep through his veins like a

poison. He looked around at the mummy cases lying like coffins in the room. Some of the lids were still on, with the painted faces staring at him. But some of the lids had slipped off onto the floor. It hadn't been like that this afternoon, when Mr. Ellerby had taken them on the tour. The mummy lids had all been shut tight.

Robbie looked down into the open cases and saw the mummies. Their faces were wrapped in white. Robbie screamed as one of the mummies rose up to stare back at him.

Then more mummies rose up. Robbie watched as their stiff arms reached up to pull themselves out of the cases. He shrank back against the wall as the mummies began to move toward him.

"No!" he screamed out. "Help me!"

But the mummies kept coming toward Robbie. They closed in on him, reaching out with their stiff, white arms.

The next morning, Mr. Arnold and Mr. Ellerby searched and searched the museum for Robbie. They looked under every statue and inside every mummy case. There was only one thing they forgot to do. They forgot to count the mummies. If they had, they would have found one more than before . . . one the size of a 12-year-old boy.

THE CORPSE'S REVENGE

Henry Archer woke with a start, feeling as though he were coming out of a long nightmare. He remembered that he had been sick for weeks, deathly sick. He remembered the doctor standing over his bed and shaking his head, as though there was no hope. The faces of his nephews were there, too, their glittering eyes staring down at his weak body. At the time, Henry's confused thoughts had cleared enough to realize that they wanted him to die, wanted him dead so they could inherit all his money.

Now Henry felt better than he had during all those long weeks of illness. The only problem he seemed to be having was a certain shortness of breath. And the night was so dark, and his bed felt unusually hard.

Henry shifted his body, feeling how stiff and cold it seemed. Then he raised his hands, which were crossed over his chest, to stretch them. To his surprise, they hit a hard wooden board only several inches above his body.

At first, Henry thought he must still be asleep and dreaming. He knew of no place like this that he'd ever been before. His hands groped around to feel what kind of place it was. The more he examined it, the more he came to realize that he was in some sort of wooden box.

The air suddenly seemed heavier around him than before. Henry's mind raced through the possibilities. He could think of no other reason why he might be in a wooden box, unless . . . unless it was a coffin.

Through the panic creeping into his brain, Henry remembered that if he were in a coffin, he would be dressed in his best clothes, not the nightclothes of a sick man. With a sinking heart, he passed his hand over the smooth silk tie lying on his chest with his big diamond stickpin fastened through it. He remembered that he had written that request in his will—that he be buried with his diamond stickpin.

Buried alive! Henry's mind sank into horror. The doctor must have thought he was dead, and buried him alive. He was *not* dead, but dead he would surely be in a few more hours.

Henry pushed up his knees against the coffin lid. It didn't budge. He thought of the six feet of earth piled on top of him. Nothing he could do would move that much weight.

A scream of despair rose in Henry's throat and echoed off the walls of the coffin. He didn't know how he could endure the slow, horrible death that awaited him now.

And then, through the thoughts that tortured him,

came a sound, a sound of something moving above him. It scratched against the dirt, with sharp, steady movements.

Every muscle in Henry's body tensed. What could be working through the ground of a graveyard with such persistence? Suddenly, Henry remembered horrible tales of graveyard rats. People said these rats were as big as cats. They dug down to freshly buried coffins. Then they chewed through the wood to get to the corpse inside. Henry shook with fear as the digging sound above him came closer and closer. He felt the air in the coffin become thicker and hotter. Now he had to face the choice of two terrible deaths.

Suddenly, there was a dull scratch against the top of his coffin lid. Henry imagined how big a rat must be to make that sound. He tried to push up against the lid, but it was fastened tight. He would have to lie there, like a helpless victim, until the rats had gnawed through the lid.

There was more scratching against the lid. Then, out of the darkness above him, Henry heard a voice.

"We've almost got it now," the voice said.

"All that's left now is to take off that lid," a second voice added.

Henry's body froze in shock. It wasn't rats that were after his body. It was grave robbers! He heard a crowbar being wedged under the coffin lid. Then, with a creak, it started to raise up.

"You reach in for the diamond stickpin," the first voice said. "Uncle Henry paid thousands for it. It must be worth a fortune by now."

"No use letting it sit on a corpse," the second said.

Just then, the coffin lid worked loose. The two young men pulled off the lid and stared down at the corpse of their uncle. And as their greedy hands reached down to grab for his stickpin, Henry Archer rose out of his coffin and pulled them down into the grave.

He left them there, screaming with terror. Then he walked back to town, brushing off the dirt that had fallen onto his diamond stickpin.

Phobia

Many people have a phobia—an unnatural fear they can't control, but Dave's phobia bordered on the fringe of madness. He would go into hysteria even at the sight of a small fieldmouse. Perhaps he had a right to be afraid, after what happened that night.

It was twilight when Dave left the small restaurant where he had eaten dinner, alone. The restaurant stood on one side of the large city park. And because it was a warm summer night, Dave decided to walk through the park to his apartment on the other side.

He started down a path overhung by leafy trees. It was surprisingly dark on the path, dark enough to make Dave feel uneasy. He quickened his pace, thinking he should get to the other side of the park as soon as possible. He had heard stories about things, unpleasant things, that happened to people in the park at night.

Then, coming out of the shaded path into an open area, he saw the sky was still light. He decided to walk a little slower, but he couldn't completely forget his uneasiness, or the stories.

He walked on through the park, toward the lake in the middle. Soon, another path loomed ahead, shaded by thick trees. Dave looked in the distance down the path. No one seemed to be on it. He looked behind him, wondering if he should turn around. By now, though, he had walked into the center of the park. There was no point in turning back.

Once on the shaded path, he could hear no sounds but the rustle of leaves. The sounds of the city were drowned out here. Dave walked on, listening to the leaves whispering in the night air. He felt as though he were a thousand miles from civilization. But then his ears picked up another sound. It wasn't a sound from the city outside and it wasn't a sound from the trees, either. He listened to his own footsteps on the cement path. He told himself that that was what he had heard.

But no, he heard it again—an echo of his own footsteps behind him. He was sure of it now; there were other footsteps, following him. Fear crept into his mind. It made his heart pound and his legs walk faster.

Soon, Dave knew he had reason to be afraid. The footsteps behind were keeping pace with his; they had quickened with his own. He kept himself from running, knowing he must not show any fear; he knew he must stay in control of himself. Forcing his legs to slow down, he realized the footsteps behind him were not slowing down. They came up from behind, quickly.

Dave couldn't control his fear any longer. He broke into a run down the path. The footsteps didn't follow right away. But then, over the pounding of his heart, he heard them hitting the pavement, fast and steady.

Ahead, Dave saw the path that went down to the lake. He knew that people more often came to the lake than to any other place in the park. He ran down a small hill toward the lake. As he rounded a corner, his heart sank. The path by the lake was deserted, too. And now, the footsteps behind him were coming down the hill and were catching up with him.

Dave looked around wildly. There was a dense area of bushes and trees to his left. He ran on a few steps and then threw himself into hiding in the bushes. Maybe, he prayed, the footsteps would go by.

It was dark now. Only a half moon penetrated the night with its mellow light. Dave heard the footsteps first, then he saw the shadow that belonged to them.

The man stopped walking 20 feet from where he was hiding. He stood silent for a minute with his back to him. Then he walked over to a bench at the lake's edge. He sat down on it.

In the bushes, Dave sat sweating. He wondered why he had ever stopped running. Nothing could be worse than this. The man must know he was hiding. Was he going to wait it out—until he couldn't stand to hide any longer? Then Dave thought of a chance. Others might walk along the path. He would jump out of the bushes then and walk with them out of the park.

He looked over at the man on the bench again. He sat calmly looking out at the lake. Something caught his eye. There was a small shadow moving along the water's edge. It stopped. Silhouetted against the sky, Dave could see the head of a large rat. He started to get up off the ground. That was always his reaction to mice—to stand on a chair, to get up off the floor in any way possible. But now, he couldn't get up. And he couldn't let loose the scream choking in his throat.

As in a bad nightmare, three more rats joined the one by the lake. Dave could see their fat shadows and their ugly rodent heads in the moonlight. And he could hear the clatter of their claws on the cement path. He wanted to scream, he wanted to run. But the bigger shadow on the bench scared him more.

The man sat still on the bench, the rats not more than five feet away from him. He must see them, Dave thought. What kind of man is he?

He switched his eyes back to the rats. They hypnotized him with loathing fear. He heard a rustle in the bushes, not more than two feet from him. He had to gag his mouth with his sweater to keep from screaming. What if a rat came up to him? What if it jumped on him with its sharp claws?

Then, with horror, Dave saw that the four rats by the lake's edge were coming toward him. Their sharp rodent noses were pointing at him. Their long tails were switching back and forth.

Dave screamed. He saw the shadow on the bench stand up. It started to come toward the bushes. Dave struggled to his feet. As he took a step backward, his foot fell into a deep hole. It was a rat's nest. Dozens of baby rats squealed in panic and crawled out of the hole around his foot. They were everywhere, scuttling away in desperation. Dave jerked his foot out of the hole. As he stepped back again, his foot landed on the soft body of a baby rat. It squealed in agony, and Dave screamed and screamed again.

Then Dave saw the shadow of the man moving closer and closer to him. He struggled to get out of the bushes, although his knees were weak with fear. Finally, he pushed his way through the thick branches and stepped onto the path going back up the hill.

The man had seen him. He came nearer. There, in the pale moonlight, Dave saw his face, and was filled with revulsion. It was the face of a huge rat, its whiskers twitching.

Dave ran. Terror, mindless terror, carried him down the path out of the park. He did not hear footsteps following behind him. All he heard was the high, unnatural squeal of rats.

Dave ran on and on until he finally escaped from the park. But as for the rat, Dave could never really escape from him. He will always be there . . . in Dave's mind.

Graveyard Dare

The four boys had dragged their sleeping bags and pillows up to the top floor of the old house. They had brought along flashlights because there wasn't any electricity in the attic. Now they were sitting around talking by the eerie glow of the lights. One of the boys—his name was Andrew—went over to the small window in one of the house's gables and peered out.

"Look, you can see that old graveyard from here," he said.

His friends, Tommy, Mark, and Richard, crowded behind him to stare out the small panes of the window.

"You can even see the tombstones," Mark said. "They're all white in the moonlight, like ghosts."

"My dad told me some old stories about that graveyard," Richard said, "when we first moved into this house. He said I should keep out of it at night."

Andrew turned to Richard with a look of disgust. "And you're probably too scared to go in there, anyway. It's only a graveyard with a bunch of dead people's skeletons a couple of feet under the ground. Do you think they're going to rise up and get you?"

The other three boys laughed nervously. Then Mark said in a low voice "Why don't you go out there right now if you think you're so brave?"

Everyone turned to watch Andrew's face. He had picked up his flashlight again, and the eerie light was shining on his features. All of a sudden, a strange grin came over his face, and he said, "Okay, I'll show you guys. I'll do it. You can watch me from up here."

"Come on, Mark was just kidding," Richard said. "And anyway, if my parents found out about this, I'd be grounded forever."

"How would they find out?" Andrew said, pulling on his sneakers.

"Listen, how will we know that you really go in?" Mark said. "You could just go down there, but never go inside the cemetery. I want proof."

"Like what?" Andrew said. "A skeleton?"

"I've got an idea," Richard said. "There's that old white birch tree that grows right in the middle of the cemetery. You've all seen it, right? It's the only birch tree growing in the whole town. So if Andrew breaks off a branch and brings it back here, we'll know from the white bark that he was inside the cemetery."

"It's a deal," Mark said.

"A deal," Andrew echoed.

Richard went down the stairs with Andrew to help him slip out the back door of the house.

"Hey, you don't really have to do this," Richard said. "We can all just forget about it, you know."

"Just go back upstairs and wait for me," Andrew said. "I'm not afraid of a graveyard at night." Then he slipped away into the shadows of the big trees that grew around Richard's house.

It was colder out than Andrew had expected. He felt the wind cut through his thin jacket as he circled around Richard's house and took the sidewalk that led to the old church. He was only a few yards away from it when the bell high in the old tower began to ring. The sound of the bell echoed through the night, over and over, one . . . two . . . three. . . . It kept up until it had struck twelve. Andrew's ears were still ringing after the bell had stopped, and his whole body seemed to be shaking. The bell's vibration had set his nerves on edge, especially when he realized that it was after midnight.

Andrew crept around the side of the stone walls of the church, heading for the low iron fence that surrounded the cemetery. Just as he drew near the gate, he heard a strange rustling sound, like animals moving in the night or branches clawing against a wall. For a second he stopped, his heart in his throat. Then he looked up and saw Richard's house in the distance. The glow of three flashlights shone in the high attic window. Andrew knew he had to go on, or he would never live it down.

The gate in the iron fence was locked, just as Andrew thought it would be. He had seen a church custodian lock it up at nightfall before. He felt the sharp tips at the top of the fence's iron bars and paused to think. Then he backed up, took a running jump, and vaulted over the fence. His feet hit the soft grass of the graveyard on the other side and seemed to sink in.

Andrew stood perfectly still for a minute, listening and looking around him. Suddenly, everything seemed different. Outside, the graveyard had looked harmless and, well, dead. But inside—inside the locked fence—it was different. The tombstones stood higher in the moonlight than he expected. Some of them were even taller than he was. They seemed to loom above him, their cold, white marble glowing in the night.

Andrew began to walk among them toward the center of the graveyard. He couldn't seem to find a path and had to walk over the soft, soggy ground. As he picked his way through the tombstones, a small, low stone caught at his foot like a trap. Andrew stopped and suddenly heard a rattling sound behind him. He whirled around, but saw nothing except a large tomb with a carved face staring back at him. The hair on the back of his neck seemed to stand up on end, and his body began to shiver even harder from the cold wind.

Andrew started to run through the graveyard, anxious to reach the birch tree and carry out his dare. He told himself that he was letting his imagination go wild. But with every step he took, he seemed to hear a strange noise behind him. Yet when he turned around to look, all he saw were the tombstones sitting like cold, silent guards over the dead.

Finally, several yards ahead, he saw the old birch tree, its white branches shining in the moonlight. Andrew knew he only had to go a little farther, and he would get what he had come for.

A low, whooo-ing sound vibrated through the air, sending chills through Andrew's body. It was an owl, he told himself, just an owl. He looked up at a tree above him and caught sight of the moon. A dark cloud was beginning to move across it. Andrew started to run faster toward the birch tree. He was almost to it when, suddenly, he tripped on a low tombstone and sprawled face down on the soft, damp ground of the cemetery. And when he looked up and pulled himself to his feet, the moon had gone under the cover of the cloud.

Andrew put both hands out in front of him and stumbled forward. It was pitch-black in the graveyard now. Then, suddenly, his right hand touched something cold and hard. He reached out for it with both hands and felt it. It must be a branch of the birch tree, he told himself. He grabbed hold of a thick part of it, and with a quick jerk, pulled. With a loud crack, it broke off in his hands. Suddenly sick with fear, Andrew pushed it under one arm and started to run.

He wasn't sure which way to go. All he cared about

was getting out of the cemetery. The strange whooo-ing sound was getting louder and louder now, and rustling and rattling sounds were all around him. He couldn't see where he was going as he ran. Twice he stumbled and fell face down on the soggy earth. But he never let go of the birch branch tucked under his arm. He was determined to show his friends that he'd completed the dare.

Andrew looked up and saw the shadowy hulk of the church looming in front of him. Then he felt his body bump right into the fence that surrounded the graveyard. He had to step back to get a running start to clear the fence. But as he backed up, he felt something grab at his coat. It tugged and tugged and seemed to try to pull him back into the graveyard. Andrew screamed and shook whatever it was off of him. Then he started to run, and just as something grabbed at the back of his neck, he jumped and cleared the fence.

He never stopped running until he reached Richard's back door. He pushed open the door and stumbled into the house, still clutching the birch branch. He ran up the three flights of stairs to the attic where his friends were waiting.

They stood there, their flashlights casting pools of light in the dark room.

"I got it," he panted. "I got it." Then he pulled the branch from under his arm and held it above his head.

The room was filled by a horrible silence. Mark, Tommy, and Richard didn't say a word. They stood staring at the thing he was holding, with looks of terror on their faces. Andrew followed their eyes up to the cold, hard object he held in his trembling hands.

And he saw that it was the arm of a skeleton . . . its bony fingers dangling down into his face.

Better Late Than Never

One morning, John O'Rourke found himself walking along a busy downtown street. He stared around in confusion at the shops and cars, having no idea why he was there or where he was going. It seemed as though he had suddenly awakened from a dream and found himself back in reality.

Coming around a corner, John looked straight ahead at the brilliant morning sun hovering low in the sky. The light almost blinded him and sent a sharp pain through his head. He pressed his hand against his forehead and then drew it away, noticing the dark red flakes on it. Strange, he thought, the flakes looked almost like dried blood.

Feeling suddenly weak, John sat down on the curb and tried to understand what was happening to him. A few seconds later, a car sped by, almost hitting him. John jerked back and tried to jump to his feet. But his body was so sore that he had trouble just standing up. He brushed off the dust from his clothes and noticed that he was wearing his best suit and a pair of highly polished shoes. But when he pulled up his coat sleeve to check the time, he found that he wasn't wearing his watch. That was the strangest thing of all. John O'Rourke never took his watch off, not even to sleep. Being on time was an obsession with him.

Now, more than ever, he felt lost and confused. What was he doing here in the middle of town? And what time was it? John began to wander aimlessly down the street. Ahead of him on the sidewalk he recognized the woman who worked in his dentist's office. He walked up behind her and tapped her on the shoulder.

"Excuse me, Mrs. Anderson, could you tell me the time? I don't seem to have my watch on."

The woman whirled around at the sound of his voice. Her eyes widened as she stared at his face. Then, with a piercing scream, she ran away down the street.

John stood frozen in place on the sidewalk, watching her flee. He asked himself why her face had contorted with fear at the sight of him. Was there something horrifying about the way he looked? Passing his hand over his face, he felt a strange bump on his forehead. And, once again, he saw the dark red flakes on his hand.

John turned and walked toward the large glass window of a store along the sidewalk. His reflection wavered in it, looking ghostly in the morning light. There seemed to be a strange, dark bruise on his forehead, and his face looked as white as the stiffly starched shirt he wore.

John walked on in the direction of the street where he lived with his wife in a small, two-bedroom house. They had never had children because John had forbidden it. He was sure that children would upset his schedule and make him late. Being late was something he could not tolerate.

Now, for some reason that he didn't understand, John felt sure that he was going to be late for an extremely important appointment. He knew his wife could tell him what it was, and she would have a warm breakfast waiting. It was odd, though; he didn't feel the least bit hungry.

Just then, a school bus rumbled by, and John stared up into its windows. Staring back at him was Lucy Potter, the little girl who lived next door. John saw her raise her hand and point at him. Her mouth was open wide as though she were laughing, or screaming. A moment later, every child's face in the windows was staring at him. John glared at the bus as it moved down the street. Obviously, he had been right not to have children if they all acted that rudely.

John found that his knees were growing weaker and weaker. He began to wish that someone he knew would drive by so that he could wave them down and ask them for a ride. John slumped against the pole of a stoplight near a street corner and stared up the road. In the distance he saw a bright yellow car that he recognized. It belonged to his secretary, Miss Spencer. John stood up straight and waved his arms. Luckily, the stoplight turned red just as the car approached.

The bright yellow car slowed down to a stop at the light, but Miss Spencer was busy looking in the rearview mirror as she put on her lipstick. John walked out into the street and tried to open the door on the passenger's side. It was locked. He rapped his knuckles on the window and peered in at Miss Spencer. She stared back at him with a look of horror on her face; then she gripped the steering wheel and pressed down on the gas pedal. The car shot forward through the red light, throwing John onto the street.

Vowing to fire Miss Spencer the first chance he got, John picked himself up and limped back to the sidewalk. His head was throbbing with pain now. He looked down at his trembling hands and saw that the skin was pale, pale as ivory, and so dry that it was almost brittle.

John staggered over to a storefront with a mirrored window and looked into it. There were dark circles around his sunken eyes. His lips seemed drained of color and wouldn't move when he tried to smile. His skin seemed to reflect the bluish color of the bruise on his forehead.

A dark fear spread through John's body, followed by the strange sense of panic. He was going to be late. And whatever appointment he had, he definitely couldn't miss it.

Behind him, John saw a telephone booth reflected in the mirror. That was the answer. He could call his wife and have her come get him. She could check his calendar and find out where it was that he had to be.

John walked as quickly as his stiff legs would carry him to the telephone booth. He slipped inside and shut the door behind him. For a moment, he was overcome by a wave of claustrophobia. The booth was so narrow; it felt almost like a coffin.

John fumbled in his pockets for a coin, but they were empty. Then he saw a shiny quarter left behind by the last person using the phone. He slipped it into the money slot and pushed the buttons for his home phone number.

The first ring of the phone sounded very, very far away. John found himself struggling to breathe. The air seemed dead in the small telephone booth. The phone in his house rang a second time. His wife usually answered right after the second ring. But, still, there was only silence, a stifling, lonely silence.

John didn't think he could stay in the narrow booth another second. His hands began to claw desperately at the handle of the door. Finally, he heard a clicking sound on the other end of the telephone line. The receiver was being picked up. A strange woman's voice said, "Hello."

"Is . . . is Mrs. O'Rourke there?" John gasped.

The woman didn't answer for a moment. Then, in an anxious voice, "Mrs. O'Rourke just left for the funeral. Haven't you heard? Her husband died two days ago in a car accident downtown."

John didn't hear any more of what the woman said. The phone slipped out of his white bony hands and dangled from its cord. Then John pushed open the door of the telephone booth and lunged out.

He would have to hurry. But he could still get to the graveyard on time.

The Gecko

Jason flicked on the light switch in his kitchen and, with a shudder, watched as all the cockroaches scurried into hiding. One slipped under the toaster. Another ran into a food cabinet. Two more disappeared behind the refrigerator.

The sight of the cockroaches made Jason's stomach turn. He had wanted to make an evening snack, but now the thought of food repulsed him. What if a cockroach was in the bread drawer? What if one of them scurried out from the refrigerator when he opened the door?

Jason flicked off the light again and crept back into his living room. He stared at the white walls of the small room, thinking how it looked like a prison cell, with its windows barred against robbers. Jason shook his head and asked himself why he had ever come to New York City. It was a cold, lonely place to be if you didn't have friends or a family. Jason thought he could almost stand the loneliness if it weren't for one thing— the cockroaches. His apartment was infested with hundreds and hundreds of them.

The roaches made him feel like a prisoner in his own home. At first, he had tried to kill them with a shoe or a newspaper. But they were always too fast, and they could always find somewhere to hide. Now, whenever he saw one, he ran away from it—from the kitchen into the living room, from the living room into the bedroom. But the roaches never left him alone. Only when he was asleep at night could Jason rid his brain of their quick, scurrying bodies.

Jason eased himself down onto his couch and carefully picked up the newspaper. Very slowly, he opened it and shook out the pages. Once, a roach had jumped out from the sports section, but tonight the paper was safe. Jason glanced over the front section, reading the headlines and editorials. Then he turned to the second section, and immediately a headline caught his eye. He leaned forward in anticipation as he read through the article. Then, with a nervous smile playing on his lips, he pulled out a notebook from his jacket pocket and wrote down an important word he had just learned: GECKO.

Jason couldn't stop thinking about the article all through work the next day. Finally, at 5:00, he left the office and hurried to the pet store that he always passed on his way home. He ran the last block just to be sure he got there before it closed. After pushing open the front door, Jason walked past the fish and hamsters and kittens in the front of the store. He went down the crowded corridor to the back, where the more exotic, and less popular, pets were kept.

There, beside a case full of snakes, Jason found the gecko. It sat alone in its glass case, staring at him with its green, popped-out eyes. Jason stared at its brown, striped body covered with scaly bumps. It was bigger, much bigger, than he thought it would be. Then suddenly, the lizard jumped up toward Jason, onto the side of the glass and stuck there. With a mixture of disgust and fascination, Jason studied the sticky pads on each of the gecko's feet. He had read about those in the article. With them, the gecko could climb up any smooth surface, even a ceiling.

The gecko's cold stare and scaly body turned Jason's stomach. But then he saw the sign hanging on the bottom of its case; it read: COCKROACH KILLER. That was why Jason had come to the pet store to find this strange animal. In the newspaper he had read that one gecko could eat ten, 20, even 30 cockroaches a night. It got its name, the article had said, from the high-pitched bark it made, especially after eating its prey. Jason took a final look at the lizard and decided he had to buy it, no matter how big and ugly it was.

A sales assistant walked by just then and offered to help him. Jason asked her if the gecko was average-sized. She admitted that it had grown quickly and was bigger than usual. But she pointed out that its size would make it an even hungrier hunter. Hesitantly,

Jason said he would buy it. A short time later, he walked out of the store with the gecko in a clear plastic carrying case.

When Jason walked into his apartment that night, he flicked on the lights and quickly looked around for the scurrying bodies that greeted him each time he came home. Ten, he counted. Ten cockroaches by the front door alone. They crept into cracks in the floor and hid under the living room furniture. Jason gritted his teeth and walked into the apartment. He set the gecko down on the small, round table that he used for eating and working. Immediately, the lizard jumped onto the side of the plastic case, staring up at him with its weird green eyes.

Jason shrugged off his coat and sat down on a chair in front of the gecko. He pulled out the newspaper article from his jacket pocket. "The Perfect Pet for the City Dweller—the Hungry Gecko," the headline read. Jason skimmed the article again to read what he was supposed to do with the gecko next. According to the writer, all he had to do was let the gecko loose in his apartment. Unlike most pets, it required no care. It fed itself on cockroaches. And, in fact, an owner seldom saw the gecko again. It came out at night—in the dark—to hunt its prey.

Jason noticed that his hands were trembling as he laid the article down on the table. He hesitated and then reached up to lift off the top of the plastic case. Just as he touched the lid, the gecko leapt up and stuck onto it. Jason jerked his hands away and stared at the ugly lizard. Suddenly, the thought of it loose in his apartment made his skin crawl. Then, out of the corner of his eye, he saw yet another cockroach scurry across the floor. That settled it.

Jason quickly reached over to the plastic case and flipped open the lid. The gecko froze for a moment under the bright light. Its scaly tail flicked back and forth. Its green eyes darted around the room. Then it suddenly sprang up and leapt onto the floor near the cockroach. Within seconds, the gecko had chased the cockroach under the refrigerator and disappeared from sight.

Jason sat silently for a moment, stunned by the thought of what he had done. Now a lizard was hiding in the dark places of his apartment, along with the cockroaches. He tried to comfort himself by picking up the newspaper article and reading it again. Finally, with wary steps, he walked into the kitchen and began to make himself dinner.

Jason took his food into the living room and sat down in front of the television to eat. He watched a long movie that took his mind off the gecko until he flicked off the set at midnight. Feeling strangely exhausted, he stumbled into this bedroom and got ready for the night.

Jason lay down in bed and shut his eyes, feeling as though he could sleep forever. As sleep began to slowly steal over his mind, a strange crunching sound suddenly broke the silence of the apartment. Crunch, crunch, crunch. Jason's body tensed, and then he sat bolt upright in bed. He strained his ears, waiting for the sound to come again. Crunch, crunch, crunch. A second later, a weird bark pierced the quiet of the night, shattering Jason's nerves. GECKO. GECKO. GECKO.

The sound of the gecko's bark made Jason's blood run cold. He fell back in bed and pulled the covers up tightly around his neck. His mind fled back to the newspaper article. It had never mentioned the horrible crunching sound that the gecko made as it ate the hard shells of the cockroaches. And it had never said how loud the gecko barked. Then Jason remembered that his gecko was bigger than most. Maybe that was why it was so loud.

Crunch, crunch, crunch. The gecko was eating another cockroach. The sound scratched at Jason's brain like fingernails against a chalkboard. He buried his head under a pillow, but even the pillow couldn't keep out the gecko's bark of triumph as it swallowed its prey.

The next morning, Jason stumbled into the bathroom and stared at his drawn, white face in the mirror. A strange glint played in his dark eyes, and his lips were pale and pulled down at the corners into an anxious grimace. He wondered if anyone would notice how he looked at work today. He wondered how he would get through the day at all.

When he finally left the office at 5:00, Jason began to follow his old route home. But as he drew closer and closer to his building, he began walking slower and slower. He didn't want to go back to his apartment, where the gecko was waiting for him in the dark.

Jason stopped at a small Italian restaurant to eat an inexpensive meal of spaghetti for dinner. Afterward, he went to see a double feature at a movie theater, which lasted for four hours. Finally, just before midnight, he pushed open the door to his apartment. As Jason flicked on the entrance light, a weird bark shattered the silence. He jumped and then looked straight up at the ceiling just above his head. The gecko's striped body was pressed there; it was crunching on a half-dead cockroach.

For a few seconds, Jason stared at it in horror. The gecko seemed to have grown during the day, and it was staring at him as though it was still hungry. Jason ran for his bedroom and slammed the door shut. He locked it behind him and stood shaking in the dark. The gecko couldn't have followed him that quickly, he told himself. He was safe here in the bedroom.

Nervously, he undressed, slipped into bed, and lay there trembling. He tried to calm his nerves and soothe his mind into sleep. There would be no crunching tonight, he told himself. No crunching. No barking. Only sleep.

Then, out of the darkness, came the sound. Crunch, crunch, crunch. Jason screamed in panic as his nerves snapped. The gecko was somewhere in the room, hunting and eating. He buried his head in the covers, but, still, he couldn't shut out the gecko's bark as it set off to find another victim in the dark bedroom.

The next morning, Jason watched his shaking hands spill coffee from his cup. Again, the gecko had kept him awake almost all night with its murderous crunching and barking. But Jason noticed that there was only one cockroach in the kitchen that morning. And there had been none in the bathroom. Slowly but surely, the gecko was stalking and killing them, one by one, through the long nights.

Just then Jason saw the gecko dart from his bedroom into the kitchen. He choked back a scream as he saw the gecko's bloated body barely squeeze under the refrigerator. It had grown even bigger during the night. Suddenly, Jason put down his coffee and stared at the wall as a new thought crept into his mind. What would happen if the gecko ran out of roaches to eat?

By the end of the week, Jason could not find one roach anywhere in the apartment, no matter how hard he searched. There were none in the refrigerator. None scurried away when he came in the door at night. None hid under the wastebasket in the bathroom or inside the magazines on his nightstand. Jason had noticed something else. The gecko's crunching had become louder and louder but less and less frequent during the night. Still, Jason had not slept. Now the silence worried him as much as the crunching had.

That evening, Jason watched television until his eyes burned with fatigue. Finally, he crept into his bedroom and lay there perfectly still in the dark. He waited and waited for the crunching sound to come. But the room was quiet, as quiet as a tomb. In his mind, Jason pictured all the places where the gecko might be. Was it lurking on the dusty floor under his refrigerator? Was it pressed up against the warm glass of his television screen? Or was it in his dark bedroom? Maybe it was crawling across the ceiling above him at this very moment. Maybe it was hungry.

Late that night, the police rushed into the apartment building to answer a call from Jason's next-door neighbor. She reported terrible screams coming from his apartment, followed by a weird crunching sound and then a blood-curdling bark.

The police broke down Jason's locked door and searched the apartment. Jason was nowhere to be found. His bed was empty. And although they looked everywhere else, the police forgot to look under the bed. There, hiding in the dark, was the bloated gecko, full at last.